D0186795

91120000415833

To Frieda and her friends

H.S.

First published in Great Britain 2014 by Egmont UK Limited
This edition published 2019 by Dean,
an imprint of Egmont UK Limited,
The Yellow Building, 1 Nicholas Road, London W11 4AN

www.egmont.co.uk

Text and illustrations copyright © Helen Stephens 2014

Helen Stephens has asserted her moral rights.

ISBN 978 0 6035 7765 9
70748/001
Printed in Malaysia

A CIP catalogue record for this book is available
from the British Library.

Betsy

Goes to School

Helen Stephens

DEAN

My name is Betsy and I have
a mummy, a daddy and a Rufus.

One day my mummy said I was
big enough to go to school.

She gave me a special new bag.

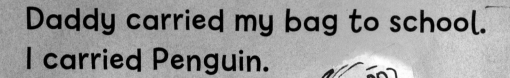

Daddy carried my bag to school.
I carried Penguin.

I saw lots of other boys and girls . . .

... but I didn't know any of them.

I held on to Daddy's buttons.

A nice lady called Lisa came to say hello.
She had a lovely red hair band.

Daddy waved goodbye.

Lisa asked if I'd like to show Penguin around.

I stayed quiet and held Penguin very tightly.

We saw the
reading corner

and a hamster.

And then . . .

. . . a girl having
a tea party!

Her cafe had cups and straws
and pretend ice cream!

I wanted to play too.

I stood very near and
watched with Penguin.

Then the girl brought Penguin
a plate with a fish on it!

She said her name was Abbie
and asked if I wanted to play.

We played in her cafe.

I was the cafe lady and Abbie
and Penguin were my customers.

Then it was story time
and Abbie shared
a cushion with me.

Penguin enjoyed
the story.

Then the mummies
and daddies
came back.

I wasn't ready to go home, but Lisa
said I could come back another day.

I asked Abbie to play dressing up with me next time.